A Friend Like Ed

Karen Wagner • Illustrations by Janet Pedersen

 ORCHARD BOOKS

D0346965

EAST SUSSEX

V CU INV NO. 16826

SHELF MARK

COPY No

BRN

DATE · .UC .UC LOC LOC LOC

COUNTY LIBRARY

To Emmy, who gives me wings – K.W.

For Mom and Dad – J. P.

Orchard Books
96 Leonard Street, London EC2A 4XD
Orchard Books Australia
14 Mars Road, Lane Cove, NSW 2066
First published in the United States of America in 1998
by Walker Publishing Company, Inc.
First published in Great Britain in 1999
This edition published in 2000
ISBN 1 84121 451 5 (hardback)
ISBN 1 84121 471 X (paperback)
Text © Karen Wagner 1998
Illustrations © Janet Pedersen 1998
The rights of Karen Wagner to be identified as the author and
Janet Pedersen to be identified as the illustrator have
been asserted by them in accordance with
the Copyright, Designs and Patents Act, 1988.
A CIP catalogue record for this book is available from the British Library
1 3 5 7 9 10 8 6 4 2 (hardback)
1 3 5 7 9 10 8 6 4 2 (paperback)
Printed in Singapore

Mildred and Ed had been friends for as long as anyone could remember
... even though some thought Ed a bit unusual.

And Mildred had to admit that Ed did have some strange
hobbies such as his enormous button collection.

Still, no one could hold a candle to Ed's homemade, fudge-frosted, triple-layer cake. Or make Mildred laugh so much that her eyes would water.

One Saturday morning Mildred said, "Let's try something different."

"Like what?" asked Ed.

"How about writing poetry? It's so romantic," answered Mildred.

"Okay," said Ed.

"Sunset is beautiful
orange and purple
Early evening
looks so . . .
yurple?"

"What's yurple?

Is yurple a word?"

Ed was the surprise hit of the
poetry class. He could find a rhyme
for anything.

"Leaves are falling
Winter's calling.
Before you know
There will be snow,
So let us shout hurray
For this warm and
sunny day."

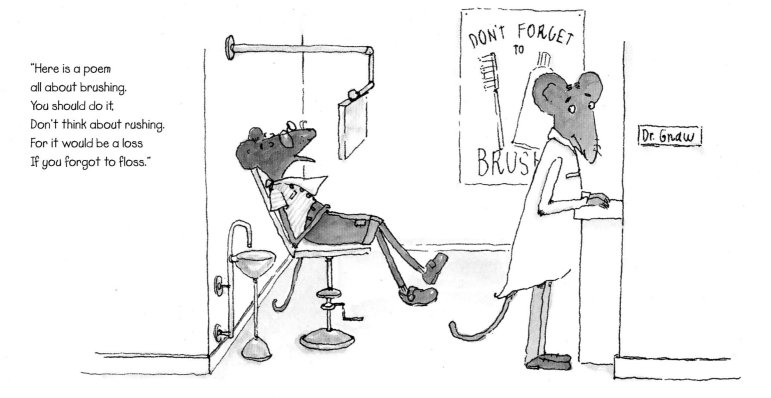

"Here is a poem
all about brushing.
You should do it,
Don't think about rushing.
For it would be a loss
If you forgot to floss."

And any place was the right place for a poem.
Soon Ed was writing poems wherever they went.

"We love to eat,
We don't use our feet.
I like bread,
but not on my head.
For dessert I'd like some pie,
Banana cream I think I'll try."

"Lemon yellow little fellow. You are sour every hour. Come along with me, I'll put you in my tea."

One day at the supermarket, Ed stopped in the middle of aisle three for a poem. Mildred felt eyes peering up from the pears. She heard snickering from behind the strawberries.

Mildred was so embarassed that she tip-toed backwards out of the store, hoping no one would notice that she was Ed's friend.

That night Mildred dreamed that her room was filled with Ed's button collection. Buttons on the floor, buttons on the chair, buttons on the walls, buttons everywhere! She wanted a friend with an ordinary sort of hobby. Then she dreamed she was ice-skating, wearing a beautiful dress. People oohed and aahed as she spun around and around.

The next day Mildred went to the ice-skating rink. She held tightly to the side because her knees wobbled. That was when she first saw Pearl. Pearl was in the middle of the rink spinning around and around. Mildred was sure no one could ever think Pearl was unusual in any odd sort of way. And she was positive Pearl had never recited poetry.

"C-c-could you teach me how to do that?" Mildred stammered.

"Of course," Pearl replied. "I can do anything. And I can do it better than anyone else."

Time passed and autumn blew in like a wind. Ed sat on top of the hill and watched the squirrels gather acorns. It felt funny without Mildred.

Pearl invited Mildred to a costume party. "We will go as a huge dragon," Pearl announced.

Pearl made a very impressive dragon. Mildred had a hard time seeing and an even harder time eating.

When winter came, Mildred and Pearl went skating on the pond. Pearl said, "Wanna see me do a triple twirl?"

"Maybe I'm ready to learn that," Mildred said.

"I think today you should just watch," Pearl said.

Ed made a fudge-frosted, triple-layer cake, even though he knew it would take forever to eat it by himself.

One morning Pearl showed Mildred all of her baby photos.

"Wasn't I the cutest baby you ever saw?" Pearl asked as she turned the pages. Mildred was busy staring out of the window at a tree. It had round, sparkling drops of ice that looked like hundreds of buttons.

Winter felt long to Ed. He sorted buttons by colour. He sorted buttons by size.

Late at night he pulled the covers up around him. He was wishing for spring, and secretly, in a voice no one could hear, he was wishing for Mildred.

When the first snow fell, Pearl and Mildred went sledding. Pearl wore her new purple scarf with matching mittens and hat. She sat on the sled and stretched out her legs.

"Where will I sit?" Mildred asked.

"I will sled down the hill," Pearl said, "And you can sled up."

Mildred felt a lump in her throat. "I'm not sledding up," she said. "I'm going home."

"Fine," Pearl said, and disappeared down the hill.

The next day Mildred woke up with a sweet tooth. "There's nothing I want more than fudge-frosted, triple-layer cake," she thought. "No one could ever make a cake the way Ed can, but I will just have to try."

Mildred looked in the pantry only to find some jars of this and cans of that but found nothing that would make a fudge-frosted, triple-layer cake. She decided to go to the supermarket.

It was cold – the kind of cold that chills you
from the inside out. Mildred dressed in all her very
warmest clothes until only a tiny bit of her face
was showing, then she set off for town.

Snow blew in Mildred's face. The wind howled. She was about to pass by the pond when she saw someone. "Who in the world would be skating on a day like today?" she wondered.

Whoever it was, he was not very good. But there was something familiar about the way he stumbled along.

"Ed!" thought Mildred, and she hid behind a tree.

Ed began to skate backwards and forwards in jerky zig-zags.

"What can he be doing?" Mildred wondered. After Ed left, Mildred peered over at the ice.

Ed was working on a new
invention for picking string beans
when the doorbell rang.

There was no one there, but on the doorstep he saw a small box and a letter.
He carefully opened the box. Inside was a pen.
The letter said:

Dear Ed,
You may think this is a pen, but it is not.
It is a thousand poems waiting to be written.
It is a pair of wings to help you fly.
Love, Mildred

Ed knocked on Mildred's kitchen door. Mildred was putting the finishing touches on a very lopsided fudge-frosted, triple-layer cake.

Ed felt suddenly shy. He looked down at his feet.

"Thank you for the pen," he said.

Mildred blushed. "I wanted to write you a poem, but I didn't know how. Maybe I need lessons."

"But you did write me a poem," Ed said. "The best kind of poem, one from the heart. That's the only lesson there is."

Mildred stood on the kitchen chair.

"Ed, oh Ed
Don't ever go.
Ed, oh Ed
I missed you so.
Ed, oh Ed
What would I do ..."

Ed interrupted. "Don't worry
Mildred, you're my best friend too."